Pilot Ollie &
Pilot Polly's
Amazing Adventures

www. planecharacters.com

Plane Characters Ltd ©

Flag Hunt!
See if you can
find all the
Christmas Crackers.

It's very early in the morning and even the birds aren't awake yet. Pilot Ollie is dressed in his smart uniform and is packing his bag for work.

He always takes his flight case to hold his maps and weather charts but today he is packing another bag full of winter clothes. He packs a big coat, a bobble hat, a long scarf and some gloves.

Outside the sky is just starting to get light and the ground is white with frost.

A plane streaks across the sky leaving fluffy white lines behind it. Today Pilot Ollie and some lucky passengers are going on a plane to meet Father Christmas.

It's December in London and everyone is getting ready for Christmas. As Pilot Ollie arrives at work he can see the sparkling decorations and the bright lights of the huge Christmas tree at the terminal.

He parks his car and walks to his briefing room.

Even the pilots briefing room has a Christmas feel. Woody Weatherman has made lots of paper snowflakes and has hung them around the walls and from the ceiling.

In the middle of the table there is a small Christmas tree that plays music and changes colour. "Good morning Pilot Ollie," says Woody Weatherman.

Pilot Ollie loves Christmas and he is very excited about today's special flight. Today Pilot Ollie is going to Lapland to meet Father Christmas.

Chris Controller walks into the room wearing a Santa hat and gives Pilot Ollie his maps for the flight. "Thank you Chris Controller," says Pilot Ollie, "I love your hat!" "Here you go," says Chris Controller, "I've got a hat for you too!"

Lapland is very close to the North Pole and it is where Father Christmas lives with his wife and hundreds of little helper elves. From Woody Weatherman's maps Pilot Ollie can see that it's going to be cold and snowy in Lapland.

"I'm glad I've brought my hat, scarf and gloves," he says.

Chris Controller's maps show Pilot Ollie how to get to Lapland.

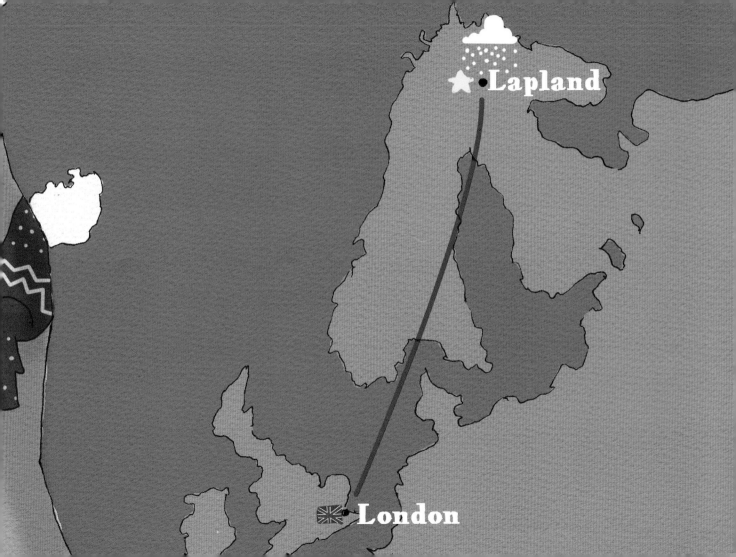

While Pilot Ollie's on the phone to Freddy Fueller ordering the fuel for the flight, Larry Loader walks into the briefing room. He is wearing his big coat as it's freezing outside.

"I've got a very special cargo for you today Pilot Ollie," he says, "It's a new sleigh for Father Christmas's village. The old one broke last week. I'll load it in the cargo hold for you."

"Thanks Larry Loader," says Pilot Ollie, "We'll take good care of it."

Out of the terminal window you can see Freddy Fueller putting fuel into the plane's wings and Larry Loader putting a huge box in the cargo hold.

Tara Turnaround comes into the terminal and makes an announcement over the loud speakers. "All passengers on today's special flight to Lapland, please board the plane now."

The passengers all line up ready to get on board the plane. "Good Morning," says Megan, "welcome aboard."

On every seat there is a special bright red Christmas cushion, a candy cane and a huge gold chocolate coin.

When all the special passengers are on board and in their seats Mike closes the plane's big door. Pilot Ollie comes out of the flightdeck. He looks funny as he is wearing the Santa hat that Chris Controller has given him.

"Good morning everyone," he says. "Are you all as excited as I am about meeting Father Christmas?"

"Yes, we are!" say the passenger's. Pilot Ollie climbs back into the flight deck, shouts "Chocks Away!" and starts the big jet engines.

"You are cleared to take off," says Chris Controller from the control tower. "Have a great time in Lapland." Pilot Ollie increases the thrust on the plane's jet engines which make a loud **ROOOAAARRR**.

The plane rumbles down the runways, leaps into the air and climbs up into the morning sky.

After a couple of hours they arrive in Lapland. Pilot Ollie brings the plane in to land. Everything is covered in snow.

The trees are white, the fields are white and the houses are covered in snow. It looks really cold.

Even the runway is covered in snow but Pilot Ollie is specially trained to land all kinds of weather.

Pilot Ollie parks the plane and speaks to the passengers again. "Welcome to Lapland," he says. "You had better put your coats, hats and gloves on because it's very cold outside."

When everyone is wrapped up Molly opens the plane's big door. The cold air and snow rushes in and it makes her shiver.

Outside in the cold and snow Larry Loader is busy supervising the unloading of the sleigh from the cargo hold. He makes sure that it is handled very carefully.

The sleigh is put on the back of a lorry and sent on its way to Christmas Village. The passengers walk through the snow to Lapland airport terminal to have their passports checked.

Outside the airport terminal are some special buses to take the passengers to Christmas Village. They are Snowmobile Buses that are specially designed for snowy countries.

Pilot Ollie, Mike, Molly and Megan get on board and sit down. When the bus is full it whisks them all off towards the North Pole and Christmas Village.

Soon the excited passengers get their first sight of Christmas Village. All of the houses are covered in bright white Christmas lights and there is a huge Christmas tree in the village square.

The streets are full of little people all wrapped up to keep warm and rushing around. "I wonder if they are Father Christmas's elves?" says Mike.

The Snowmobile Bus pulls up at the station. "Tervetuola!" which is Finnish for "Welcome!" says the tour guide who is waiting for them at the station.

The tour guide takes them to the town square and right by the huge Christmas tree is an ice skating rink.

There are big plastic penguins that beginners can use to help them around the ice. Pilot Ollie has skated before so he zooms off around the rink. Mike, Megan and Molly all hold hands. It's very slippery on the ice.

After the ice skating the special passengers have some lunch and then they are going on a sleigh ride to the reindeer park. The husky dogs are barking and are ready to pull the sledge.

Larry Loader arrives on a big truck that is carrying the sleigh that had been on the flight over. The elves help unload the sleigh, attach the huskies and they are ready to go.

At the reindeer park there are hundreds of reindeer. Some are eating hay, some are scratching their backs on the pine trees and a few of them are in a special pen with a sign on it saying Christmas Sleigh.

The Reindeer all have a bell around their neck and it sounds very Christmassy. One of the reindeer in the pen has a red nose.

"I wonder if that is Rudolph?" says Molly. "Yes it is!" says the tour guide, "and that one over there is Prancer."

Behind the reindeer park, hidden amongst the pine trees is a huge building with the words "Toy Factory" written on the side. Next to the factory is a little house with small windows and a steep roof.

The roof was covered in snow and the front of the house was decorated with white lights. "That is where Father Christmas lives," says the guide.

"Let's go and meet him." Megan is very excited about meeting Father Christmas. She has her Christmas list in her pocket.

The guide walks Pilot Ollie and Megan to Father Christmas's house and opens the door. They step inside and see a room full to the roof with bulging sacks of presents.

Father Christmas has lots of elves that help him and they were running around getting ready for the big day. Some were pushing trolleys full of presents and some were going through a door marked "Toy Factory - Secret – No Entry".

Toy Factory
SECRET
NO ENTRY

Next to the Toy Factory door was another door. Megan pushes the door open a bit and there sat in a rocking chair by the open fire is Father Christmas.

"Hello," says Father Christmas. "I hope you are enjoying your day in Christmas Village? Have you been good this year?" "Yes" says Megan, "I have been very good indeed."

Father Christmas leans forward and says, "Have you made a Christmas list for me?" Megan gives Father Christmas their list and he puts it in his pocket.

"I'll see what I can do," says Father Christmas, "No promises though!"

The day has been amazing but unfortunately it's time to fly home. The tour guide has arranged for the snowmobile bus to pick all the passengers up from Father Christmas's house and whisk them back to the airport.

Pilot Ollie, Mike, Megan and Molly jump onto the bus. "Did you enjoy your day?" Pilot Ollie says. "It's been an amazing adventure," says Mike, "and I even got to meet Father Christmas!"

Back at the airport the ground staff have cleaned the plane and filled the wing tanks with fuel. Pilot Ollie collects some new maps and charts from the local briefing room and programmes the plane's computers with the route home.

The special passengers go through the airport terminal and then get on the plane. It's time to head home and everyone's tired after such an exciting day.

Also Available

www.planecharacters.com

Also Available

About the Author

In 1997 Rob successfully applied for sponsorship to become a commercial airline pilot and then spent 18 months training, initially in South Australia and then finally in Prestwick, Scotland.

After gaining his wings he spent his first five years flying as a First Officer on short haul routes in Europe. Rob then moved on to larger aircraft on long haul routes world-wide. More recently Rob gained promotion to Captain in 2007 and then a subsequent promotion to Training Captain in 2012.

Rob initially wrote the Pilot Ollie and Pilot Polly books for his own children as they were always interested in the places that he had been to and the sights that he had seen. Hence in an effort to share these experiences with his children and also other children with similar enquiring minds he decided to publish them. The books are written to be fun, informative and engaging along with being educational.

For more information visit www.planecharacters.com